The Three Bears

as told by Mabel Watts

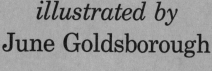

illustrated by
June Goldsborough

GOLDEN PRESS
Western Publishing Company, Inc.
Racine, Wisconsin

Seventh Printing, 1980

Once upon a time three bears plumped themselves down before three bowls of porridge piping hot from the pot.

"Ouch!" growled the great big Papa Bear, in his gruff, growly voice. "I burned my tongue!"

"And I burned my nose!" squeaked roly-poly Baby Bear, in his teddy-bear voice.

The middle-sized Mamma Bear blew at the steam. "I'm so sorry!" she said, in her lady-bear voice.

The three bears fanned their tongues. They ran for the water bucket.

"Let's take a walk while our porridge cools," said Papa Bear.

"Walking is good for the appetite," said
Mamma Bear. "And we *need* exercise!" So off
they waddled into the woods.

A few minutes later, a little girl named
Goldilocks came skipping along toward the
cottage of the three bears.

She was making a crown of daisies to wear
on her golden hair.

Then she smelled the porridge!

"Hi!" she called through the open door. "Is anyone home?"

There was no answer. So Goldilocks walked in and looked around. She saw the three bowls of porridge cooling on the table. "It looks good," she said. "It smells good. And I'm hungry."

First Goldilocks tasted the porridge in Papa Bear's bowl. "Too hot!" she said. "Too salty!"

She tasted the porridge in Mamma Bear's medium-sized bowl. "Too cold!" she said, shaking her head.

She sipped the porridge in Baby Bear's wee, tiny bowl. "Just right!" said Goldilocks. She ate it all.

In a cozy corner Goldilocks saw three rocking chairs.

First she tried the big, roomy one belonging to Papa Bear.

"Too hard!" said Goldilocks.

Next she tried the middle-sized chair belonging to Mamma Bear.

"Bright and pretty," said Goldilocks, "but too soft!"

She tried Baby Bear's little red rocker.
"Just the right size!" said Goldilocks. But
she rocked too hard, and she rocked too fast.
And . . .

snap, crack, clatter — down went the chair into little pieces.

"I'd try to fix it," sighed Goldilocks, "if I weren't so sleepy."

Upstairs under the eaves stood three beds
in a row.

First Goldilocks tried Papa Bear's enormous,
big bed.

"Bumpy as a sack of pebbles!" said Goldilocks. "And much too hard!"

Mamma Bear's middle-sized bed was stuffed full of fluffy thistledown. *Plop!* Goldilocks sank down deep into the middle.

"Too soft!" She sneezed. She could hardly climb out!

But Baby Bear's little, wee bed felt comfy
and cozy. Goldilocks yawned.

"This bed is just right!" she whispered
drowsily.

And soon — ho-hum — she was sound asleep.

And that's when the three bears got back from their walk, smiling and carrying honeycombs.

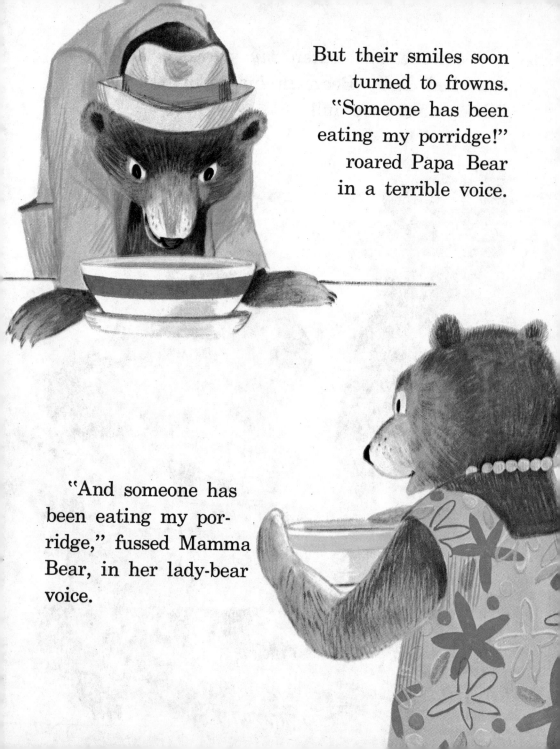

But their smiles soon
turned to frowns.
"Someone has been
eating my porridge!"
roared Papa Bear
in a terrible voice.

"And someone has
been eating my por-
ridge," fussed Mamma
Bear, in her lady-bear
voice.

"Someone has eaten *my* porridge all up,"
squeaked Baby Bear, in his teddy-bear voice.
"Every last spoonful!"

Papa Bear thumped into the next room. "Someone has been sitting in my chair!" he thundered.

"Mine, too!" said Mamma Bear. "I wonder who."

"Someone has been sitting in *my* chair," sobbed Baby Bear, "and broken it all to pieces!"

"A burglar!" said Mamma Bear.

"A giant!" said Baby Bear.

"Wait till I get my paws on him!" growled Papa Bear.

Up the stairs, on tiptoe, went the three bears.

"Someone has been sleeping in my bed!" declared Papa Bear.

"Someone has been sleeping in my bed. Why, the covers are all mussed up!" said Mamma Bear.

"Someone has been sleeping in *my* bed," squealed Baby Bear. "AND LOOK! HERE SHE IS!"

"It isn't a burglar!" said Mamma Bear, coming closer.

"It isn't a giant!" whispered Baby Bear.

"Just a tired little girl!" said Papa Bear.

Goldilocks opened her eyes and blinked. Up she jumped, screaming, "Bears!"

Down the stairs she ran, her golden hair flying.

Out the door, through the woods — away, away, away. . . .

"I wanted that little girl to stay and play," said Baby Bear sadly.

"She'll come this way again," promised Mamma Bear.

And in the end the three bears did get their breakfast.